It's Mine!

One day, Milo, Doodles and Izzles were playing at being farmers.
"Can I borrow Lamby for our game?" Milo asked Fizz.
"No," said Fizz, hugging the toy lamb. "Lamby's mine!"

"I'll give her back," Milo promised, grabbing Lamby's leg.
Fizz pulled, and Milo pulled, then suddenly...

...Lamby's leg fell off! Fizz screamed, and Judy ran over to see what had happened.

"He broke my Lamby," wept Fizz.

"I didn't mean to hurt Lamby," Milo explained. "I just wanted to borrow her."

"I can mend Lamby," Judy told them, "but you should be more careful, Milo, and you should share your toys, Fizz."

"Oh dear!" Doodles muttered. "Milo might break something of mine."
He put all his toys on his beanbag, and sat down beside them.

"I'll take Lamby to hospital to get better," said Fizz, when Judy had finished sewing on the toy's leg.

Doctor Fizz and Nurse Bella tucked up
Lamby in the playhouse.

Jake fetched her supper, and Milo looked for one of his favourite
books to read to her.

Milo found the book on Doodles' beanbag, but Doodles barked, "No, Milo, it's mine. Mine, all mine!"

"Max!" Milo called. "Doodles won't let me have the book."

"You're being selfish," Max told Doodles. "You remind me of the story of The King Who Wanted the Moon."

Doodles didn't know the story, so the Tweenies decided to act it out, with Doodles as the king.

"Once upon a time," Max began, "there was a king who wanted to own everything he saw. He would walk around all day long, saying, 'That's mine!'"

"One night the king gazed up at the moon and said, 'I must have the moon. It must be mine, all mine!' He wondered how he could reach it."

"Then he had an idea. He ordered all the carpenters in the land to make him a very long ladder."

"The king climbed right to the top of the ladder," Max continued, as Doodles bounded up the climbing frame steps.

"But he still couldn't reach the moon, so he ordered his people to bring him all the boxes in the land."

"The king built a tall tower with the boxes, and climbed up as high as he could go. But he still couldn't reach the moon."

"So he ordered his people to pull out one box from the bottom of the tower and pass it up to him.
   They did as he commanded..."

"...and the tower collapsed!
The king fell down and landed
with a bump," chuckled Max.
"His crown slipped over one eye
and everyone laughed. But he'd
learnt his lesson, and never
asked for the moon again."

Doodles came whooshing down the slide.

"Yes," said Bella. "He learnt that you can't have everything."
"Are you going to share your things from now on?" Milo asked Fizz and Doodles.

"Yes," laughed Fizz. "I don't want to be like that king!"
"I suppose so," Doodles sighed.

But later, when Jake gave Doodles some biscuits to cheer him up,
Doodles licked his lips and said...

"Mine, all mine!
I mean, have a biscuit, everyone!"

The End